Blank Canvas

BLANK CANVAS

a play in two acts

by Alex Sauer

ISBN: 978-0-9998621-6-2   Printed in U.S.A

IMPORTANT BILLING AND CREDIT REQUIREMENTS

All producers of *BLANK CANVAS* must give credit to the Author of the Play in all programs distributed in connection with performances of the Play, and in all instances in which the title of the Play appears for the purposes of advertising, publicizing or otherwise exploiting the Play and/or a production. The name of the Author must appear on a separate line on which no other name appears, immediately following the title and must appear in size of type not less than fifty percent of the size of the title type.

CHARACTERS

KENNEDY HANNAH SHAY- a girl in her late twenties/early thirties

MARIE SHAY- Kennedy's mother

JOSEPH SHAY- Kennedy's father

PEYTON SHAY- Kennedy's sibling

MACKENZIE WILLIAMS- Kennedy's friend

THEO HUMPHREY- Kennedy's friend/lover

YOUNG KENNEDY- the younger version of Kennedy, age 7

YOUNG PEYTON- the younger version of Peyton, age 4

ALMA HUMPHREY- a girl in her early twenties, Theo's cousin

GINA- a waitress at a café in Spain

THE ARTISTS- depictions of the famous artists CEZANNE, KAHLO, VAN GOGH, POLLACK, PICASSO, and RENOIR.

CURATOR- male or female, will only be heard in voiceovers

MUSEUM WORKER-works at the entrance and exit of the museum

CASTING NOTES

The following characters can be combined at director's discretion - Kennedy/Young Kennedy, Peyton/Young Peyton, and Museum Worker/Gina

Peyton Shay can be played by any actor. Please adjust pronouns per actor's preference.

The Curator role can be anyone in the cast as the curator is only heard in voiceover.

The Artists can be casted individually, double casted, or visual. Please use creative liberty.

SETTING

In the Philadelphia Museum of Art, in Kennedy's childhood home, Kennedy's New York apartment, a club, and a café in Spain.

The play will take place in various settings, but all of these settings will take place within a frame that frames the stage during Act I. The frame should be able to be walked over or through easily. The set inside the frame should be simple relying on movable furniture, such as a table, chairs, etc. The lighting of acting outside of the frame should be very bright, with no color. Similar to a lighting of a gallery, while lighting within the frame could take on any form with varied textures in color depending on the setting and mood.

The play will continue in these various settings, but in Act II it will be simpler. The foreground will be white. The stage will rely less on movable objects and more on visuals in these scenes.

ACT I

SCENE I
SCENE II
SCENE III
SCENE VI
SCENE V
SCENE VI
SCENE VII
SCENE VIII
SCENE IV
SCENE V

ACT II

SCENE I
SCENE II
SCENE III
SCENE IV
SCENE V
SCENE VI
SCENE VII

ACT I
SCENE I

(A small crowd is in a line off stage. A spotlight is on ALMA who is nervously playing with her ticket. The stage should be very bright, white, and boxy at this moment as Alma enters the gallery. We should be able to see Cézanne's The Large Bathers at center stage.)

MUSEUM WORKER
Please only tickets before 11:30. Please step forward. If you have an 11:45 ticket, please wait another 10 minutes.

>   *(MUSEUM WORKER waves the crowd*
>   *forward and puts an audio guide over each*
>   *person's head. Another scans the ticket.*
>   *ALMA steps forward with the crowd.)*

Please follow the exhibit through here. Please press the number one to hear an introduction to the exhibit.

ALMA
Do you have a brochure? They were out at the beginning.

MUSEUM WORKER
Please follow the exhibit Miss. You can get a brochure at the end. You are holding up the crowd. (*Pauses*) Please press number one to hear an introduction folks! Press the number one. (*Helps some of the folk in the line*)

>   *(ALMA sighs and puts the*
>   *headphones on. She presses one.)*

CURATOR
(V.O)
Welcome to the Philadelphia Museum of Art! I am the
curator of the Museum and am so glad to present this
collection of work for you. We are thrilled to present
upcoming artists next to some of the most prized pieces in
the world. One of our upcoming artists, Hannah Shay,
specially narrates our *Exploring the Artist* exhibit. To learn
more about Hannah Shay, please press 101 after this
message. Please continue into the exhibit to Paul Cézanne's
The Large Bathers and press 2 to hear more about Cézanne
and his contemporary works.

ALMA

Play.

> *(ALMA hangs back as the crowd
> continues forward to the Cézanne
> piece.)*

(Director's note: As Kennedy's voice over plays,
Alma will become more interested in Kennedy's
work over other artists. At this moment, the
Cézanne piece should fade and the stage should
shift into the frame that will present Kennedy's
work. Alma should fall back and throughout the
play, she may walk the aisles or sit on a cushioned
stool in the center of the theater. When Alma is
speaking a spotlight should be on her, but when she
is not other actors should be around. Alma should
not be on stage until the very last scene of Act I.)

KENNEDY
(V.O.)
Hi. I'm Hannah Shay. I used to come to the Philadelphia Museum of Art all the time when I was teen. It's an honor to have my own work next to some of my favorite artists. I bet you are wondering what inspired these artists, and unfortunately we don't always know. That's why I'm here. In conjunction with the Philadelphia Museum of Art, I offered to give you, the listener, insight into my paintings. Continue on to the Cézanne piece. On the opposing wall, you will find my first piece. To keep listening to my commentary throughout the exhibit, please follow the numbers printed in red. For other commentary from the curator and other artists, please follow the numbers printed in black. I hope you keep listening and enjoy your visit.

ALMA
Screw Cézanne. This is something. (*Scans for a number*) 2-0-1.

ACT I
SCENE II

(ALMA is in the aisles looking over the painting. The painting should look layered with the lighting and set pieces.)

KENNEDY
(V.O.)
What do you notice that's different from the other artists in this exhibit?

ALMA
There is a lot of stuff happening. Everywhere.

KENNEDY
(V.O.)
Some people say it looks muddy. There is no focal point. And they would be right. Focus on the right of the painting.

ALMA
I just see a bunch of red lines. Maybe some faces?

KENNEDY
(V.O.)
Step back a bit. Don't try to distinguish too much and let me tell you one of my embarrassing stories. (*Laughs*)

(*YOUNG KENNEDY enters stage right. She sits on the floor with coloring books and crayons. She starts coloring the picture. MARIE comes in with bags of groceries and sets them on the table.*)

MARIE
What are you coloring sweetheart?

YOUNG KENNEDY

A bear.

MARIE

What kind of bear?

YOUNG KENNEDY

A brown bear. See?

MARIE

Honey, if it's a brown bear why are you coloring the bear blue?

YOUNG KENNEDY

Just because he is a brown bear, doesn't mean he has to be brown. He wants to be blue.

MARIE

Brown bears are brown. Why don't you start over on this page?

> (MARIE turns the page and then puts a pot of water on the stove.)

YOUNG KENNEDY

Fine.

> (Kennedy picks up a red crayon and colors in an elephant.)

MARIE

But darling, elephants are gray!

YOUNG KENNEDY

Mom. She is sunburned!

> *(JOSEPH enters taking off*
> *his gardening gloves.)*

JOSEPH

Nice elephant!

MARIE

Don't encourage her. Tell her elephants are gray!

JOSEPH

Marie. She is just coloring. Who cares what color the elephant is?

MARIE

Dinner will be ready soon.

> *(MARIE puts the pasta in boiling*
> *water and looks through the grocery*
> *bags for the pasta sauce. She pulls it*
> *out and then gets three plates out.)*

JOSEPH

Come on kiddo. Let's get this cleaned up before your mother has a fit.

> *(YOUNG KENNEDY and JOSEPH*
> *exit the stage with the materials.*
> *Marie exits the opposite side.)*

(KENNEDY and THEO enter. Theo
starts putting pasta on a plate.
Kennedy finishes putting the rest of
the groceries away and clearing the
table. Theo puts down the plates.)

KENNEDY
(V.O.)
Now that's only one story. But look again as I tell you this
other story...

THEO
That's your embarrassing story?

KENNEDY
Yes! The whole plate of pasta fell into my lap. My dad
wouldn't stop calling me the red elephant in the room. My
mom was so pissed.

THEO
You, the red elephant in the room. Haha. How fitting. I'm
sure *you've* done something more embarrassing than *that*.

KENNEDY
What makes you think I'd tell you?

ALMA
So what are the other embarrassing stories?

KENNEDY
(V.O.)
If you look closely you will see other embarrassing stories.
Like in the left corner, the time I tripped in front of my
crush or in the center when I gave a speech and stuttered.
My next painting will be beside Vincent Van Gogh's

Sunflowers. Press 1-0-3 to hear more about Vincent Van Gogh.

ALMA

And what about yours? Where is that number? (*Sighs*) I guess it wouldn't kill me to listen to Van Gogh. 1-0-3.

ACT I
SCENE III

ALMA

I would have rather heard about a different Van Gogh painting. (*Sits down*) Now Kennedy, what's with this title? Crushing? I don't get it. You better explain because all I see is a mopey dog over there. (*Motions to one of the corners*) 2-0-2.

KENNEDY
(V.O.)

All of my pieces are very autobiographical. Some artists paint sceneries or nudes or still lifes, but for me, I like to paint what happens. I have a sibling. I was trying to put myself in their shoes when I painted this...

>*(PEYTON and KENNEDY are sitting on steps within the frame.)*

KENNEDY

I'm sorry, Peyton.

PEYTON

I hate him.

KENNEDY

Don't say that.

PEYTON

Whatever.

>*(In the foreground, MARIE and JOSEPH are in the kitchen. YOUNG KENNEDY and YOUNG PEYTON are sitting playing a board game.)*

KENNEDY
(V.O.)
If you look slightly to the right of this, you will see two
figures. Those are my parents.

ALMA
But everything looks fine in this painting! Except the
colors. Shouldn't this be angrier if it's in your sibling's
shoes? I would've just painted a whole canvas red, not
purple!

KENNEDY
(V.O.)
Now put yourself in my father's shoes. Look for his actions
in the painting.

JOSEPH
I told you I was sorry.

MARIE
You slept with her.

JOSEPH
I...I...I know.

MARIE
You slept with the babysitter, Joseph. You cheated.

JOSEPH
I know.

MARIE
WHAT WERE YOU THINKING?

JOSEPH
She told me she loved me. I don't know. I wasn't. I wasn't thinking. It just happened, okay?

MARIE
Psh! Okay? What and I don't tell you I love you?

JOSEPH
Never. You're always sneaking off! Kennedy keeps asking me who that man she always sees you with! The car doesn't break every damn week Marie!

MARIE
What are you accusing me of?

JOSEPH
You're sleeping with him. With JEFF! Our mechanic!

MARIE
And? You cheated. YOUR LOUSY ASS CAN GET OUT OF THIS HOUSE! I'll sleep with who I want.

JOSEPH
That's not fair. You know…you know I try. It was one time! An accident!

MARIE
Try? It wasn't a fucking accident! The home improvement store is closing in town anyways! Nobody comes here. You won't be the manager anymore anyways. This town is going to shit and you know it. We are barely making ends meet.

JOSEPH
We can move.

11

MARIE

I am taking the kids to my parent's house.

JOSEPH

You can't just take the kids to Florida. Those are my kids too!

MARIE

Please stop trying to act like a father because *you* messed up. KIDS! Clean this shit up! What did I tell you two five minutes ago! We have to drive all the way to Pittsburgh to get the plane!

> *(MARIE exits with the car keys walking through KENNEDY and PEYTON. JOSEPH leans down and helps the kids pick up. He rests the board game on the table.)*

JOSEPH

Let's go before your mom starts yelling again.

YOUNG PEYTON

Dad, are we going to go fishing next weekend? You promised.

JOSEPH

Of course.

> *(JOSEPH smiles sadly at YOUNG PEYTON. YOUNG PEYTON and YOUNG KENNEDY exit past KENNEDY and PEYTON. JOSEPH reenters the house. Lighting should change to show time passing within the house. JOSEPH changes shirts*

and ties up some boots. He continues shifting around the dining area/living area, while KENNEDY and PEYTON talk. He eventually sits down to write a letter.)

KENNEDY

We can always go visit Dad.

PEYTON

Why would I want to go visit that asshole? He abandoned us and it sucks out there.

KENNEDY

He's not that bad. You know how Mom talks about him. He wants to see you. Then we can go visit colleges in Pittsburgh. There are some good ones out there. I think you'd really like…

PEYTON
(Cuts Kennedy off)
I don't want to go to school out there.

KENNEDY

Where are you going to go then? You graduated a year ago. I can't keep helping you and mom.

PEYTON

I'll figure it out. Me and mom are happy in Philly!

KENNEDY

You don't even have a job.

PEYTON

Just go back to New York alright?

KENNEDY

Come on.

PEYTON

Lay off.

(PEYTON exits.)

JOSEPH

Clarion County hasn't changed much. Thanks for the painting of your trip to England. I hung it above the couch. Remember that ugly patch of wallpaper? The painting covered it beautifully. I've started doing landscaping at one of the colleges. It's an hour drive, but it's the best job offer I've had in a long time. Here is 50 dollars to add to that savings account for your sister/brother. They will need it when they go to college. Call me when you are back. I want to hear all about it. Love, Dad. *(Pauses)* I should have fought harder all these years.

> *(JOSEPH grabs his jacket and exits dropping the letter in KENNEDY'S hands. They should not make eye contact. KENNEDY fidgets with the letter)*

KENNEDY
(V.O.)

In this painting, I used the letters of my father as a base and then painted over them. Some places you can see his tight cursive writing and other places you can't. I wanted to capture how I felt crushed by the later divorce of my parents, but also how my father and sister/brother felt crushed. One being angry and the other being sad. Red. Blue. As the layers came together, some of it became purple. The next painting will be next to Frida Kahlo's *The Two Fridas*. Press 1-0-4.

ALMA
Hmmm. I think I'm starting to get this.

ACT I
SCENE IV

ALMA

You know, you kind of are doing something like Frida.
Like she showed how she was torn between her two selves.
And then she did all those self-portraits. Whatever. 2-0-3.

KENNEDY
(V.O.)

I was lucky to travel after college and my friend and I lived
a year in Spain. She was writing freelance, while I worked
in a hostel. When I didn't have shifts, we sat in a café and
chatted. We swore we would speak Spanish, but soon
learned it wasn't that easy.

(MACKENZIE and KENNEDY are
sitting in a café in Spain talking.)

GINA

¿Café con leches?

MACKENZIE

Sí. Y....y... una tostada con mermelada.

KENNEDY

Solo un café con leche hoy.

(GINA exits for the coffee.)

MACKENZIE

I have the *ganas* to go somewhere new. Where should we
go this *fin de*?

KENNEDY

What does the magazine need?

16

MACKENZIE

They are always looking for something coastal. The playa
sells.

(GINA reenters with the coffee.)

GINA

Chicas! Castellano. Si queréis aprender…habláis! (*Laughs*)

KENNEDY

Si quieres ir a…alguien lugar…donde iría, Gina? Ella tiene
que escribir…sobre una vacación por una revista.

GINA

A mi casa. En Romania.

MACKENZIE

No eres castellano?!

GINA

No chica. Está aquí por mi amor. Amor te vuelve loco. Si
quieres más café, dime.

KENNEDY
(V.O.)

We had been in that café for weeks and we thought Gina
was a Spaniard. But she was just like us. Working and
working to stay there. Well we were not there for
love…well at least not that kind of love. Gina taught us
something.

ALMA

Well, clearly! But what? This seems a bit sappy.

KENNEDY
(V.O.)
Look at the title closely. Humbling. What do you think of
when you hear that?

ALMA
(*Plops on the stool dramatically*)
I think of those stupid motivational speakers from high
school who come from humble beginnings.

KENNEDY
(V.O.)
I usually get pretty positive vibes from the word, but when
we encountered Gina, I started wondering about the real
feeling. When you are humbled by something, you are
changed by it. But are you not embarrassed too?

ALMA
I know this is an art exhibit, but you are getting a bit
philosophical. Please tell me there is something more to
this. How about what is happening in the other corner? The
dark one! I can't even make out anything!

KENNEDY
(V.O.)
So you know how sometimes, you are working on
something and you spill coffee all over it? Well, that's what
happened here, but with paint. I was so focused on
capturing the warm fuzzies of humbleness that when I went
to put details in with this dark purple, I knocked the cup
over. I almost just painted over everything, but let it dry
and left it. It reminded me of the first time I felt humbled.

(KENNEDY walks down a hallway to the shower. She is in a robe and is carrying a tote of shampoo and body wash. MACKENZIE is combing her hair and about to blow dry her hair.)

KENNEDY

Hi.

(KENNEDY gets in a shower. She closes the door. Another college kid enters obnoxiously. MACKENZIE leaves down the hall. As soon as she exits, the college kid takes KENNEDY'S robe that is hanging and runs down the hallway)

MACKENZIE

What the hell do you think you are doing? Give me that girl's robe!

(The college kid hesitates until MACKENZIE lurches at him/her. Mackenzie walks back to the bathroom where KENNEDY is peeking out of the stall.)

MACKENZIE

Some kid stole your robe but I got it back. (*Hands KENNEDY the robe*)

KENNEDY

I would have hid here all night.

(KENNEDY picks up her caddy and ties the robe securely before almost leaving. MACKENZIE stops   her.)

MACKENZIE

Are you going to say thank you?

KENNEDY

Thank you?

KENNEDY
(V.O.)

Needless to say, the next time I showered, Mackenzie stole the robe of the hook. Wrapped in a too small towel, I knocked on her door and apologized. No one had ever taught me to be grateful, but Mackenzie was bold enough to make a fool out of me to teach me. I didn't think to include that moment until I spilled that paint, but it was a vital part of my memories related to humbleness.

ALMA

You're doing portraits of memories almost? But your titles still make no sense. I'm sure if I had the brochure I'd know why. Stupid worker.

KENNEDY
(V.O.)

Please continue to the next piece Pablo Picasso's *Girl Before A Mirror*. Press 1-0-5.

ACT I
SCENE V

ALMA

This one. This one is dark. Lots of texture. I have to hear
this story. 2-0-4.

KENNEDY
(V.O.)

This was one of the hardest pieces to paint. I had been
through break ups before, but never one as complicated as
the one depicted here. Even as I tell the story, I still get
worked up. Let's start off slow. Look at the pale yellow
section.

*(KENNEDY and THEO are
sitting at their dining room
table, eating silently. The
lighting should be warm and
yellowish.)*

THEO

Could you say something?

KENNEDY

It was a long day.

THEO

That's all?

KENNEDY

A pipe broke in the kitchen at the hostel.

THEO

I'm not talking about the hostel.

KENNEDY

Mackenzie and I are going out tonight.

*(KENNEDY gets up and washes her
dish. THEO gets up and rests his
hand on her shoulder.)*

THEO

When are we going to talk about what happened between
us?

KENNEDY
(Turns around)

We're not. I have to get ready. Entertain Mackenzie when
she gets here.

(KENNEDY exits.)

ALMA

Well that doesn't seem fair. What happened?

KENNEDY
(V.O.)

Lots of times, we don't know what to say. How to talk
about our feelings. I happen to put it on canvas. Look to the
bright red spot and keep listening.

THEO

Will do.

*(THEO washes his dish and
puts it on the drying rack. He
wipes the table down.)*

*(MACKENZIE knocks loudly,
and then enters.)*

MACKENZIE

Is she getting ready?

THEO

Yeah.

MACKENZIE

What's bumming you out? It's not like you to pass on a night out?

THEO

Didn't realize I was invited.

MACKENZIE

I'm only in town once in a blue moon. I have to see my favorite couple.

THEO

She didn't tell you?

MACKENZIE

You didn't. You decided now was a good time to break up with her? What the hell were you thinking?

THEO

She wouldn't talk to me.

MACKENZIE

You know how she is. You two live together. Let her and I have some girl talk. I'll shoot you a text once she loosens up.

THEO

Fine.

MACKENZIE

HURRY UP!

(KENNEDY enters)

KENNEDY

Hush. I'm ready.

MACKENZIE

Is that the dress I sent you from London?

KENNEDY

Of course.

MACKENZIE

I knew it'd look stunning. Now let's go get drunk! The club is waiting for this girl to let loose!

THEO

And you'd think she never partied a day in her life.

KENNEDY
(Smiles at Theo)

Let's go Mack!

(MACKENZIE and KENNEDY leave laughing. THEO runs his hand through his hair. He picks up a pile of manuscripts. He goes to sit in a chair by a window. The chair should be off to the side. He turns the lamp to the side of the chair. On the stage behind him, the GIRLS enter the nightclub. The lighting should be more blue and purple toned to contrast the warm lighting of the apartment.)

KENNEDY
(V.O.)
Look at the dark spots on the canvas. See the flecks of
light. The shadows.

ALMA
I see them. I just don't see why you are not giving the
details on your break up.
(*beat*)
I guess this is an art museum and not a soap opera.

> (*ALMA sighs and continues
> listening. She sits down on a couch
> in the aisle looking intently at the
> painting as if to try to figure it out.*)

MACKENZIE
I'm thrilled. I get to do reviews of Southern France cuisine
for my next article.

KENNEDY
Take me with you.

MACKENZIE
Haha. If I could I would. But who would run the hostel?

KENNEDY
I think it's time for a remodel of that place.

MACKENZIE
You've been saying that for years.

KENNEDY
A pipe broke this morning, I don't think I have a choice.

(Both laugh as they take their margaritas off the bar top.)

MACKENZIE

Maybe it will be a good thing.

KENNEDY

Don't tell him. But I'm finally moving out. (*Drinks rest of margarita*)

MACKENZIE

Because you two broke up?

KENNEDY

He told you!

MACKENZIE

He didn't have to. How long ago?
                    (Kennedy orders another drink)
How long ago?

KENNEDY

A month...Two months.

MACKENZIE

TWO MONTHS?

KENNEDY

He wanted to see other people. I don't want to talk about it. I want to have fun tonight before you fly off to Southern France.

MACKENZIE

Fine. That's not what he told me. I'll cut you some slack this *one time*. But you owe me a real talk over Skype! Shots!

ALMA
I can't believe your friend would just let you off the hook.

KENNEDY

Shots!

>(KENNEDY and MACKENZIE down
>three shots each. They go to the
>dance floor and dance. The music is
>loud and thumping.)

>(THEO picks up his phone and sends
>a text.)

>(KENNEDY and MACKENZIE are
>taking selfies. MACKENZIE runs off
>to the bar for more drinks.
>KENNEDY sees she has a text. She
>quickly replies and puts her phone
>away. Her mood shifts.)

>(THEO phone buzzes. He sighs.)

>(MACKENZIE comes back with two
>drinks. KENNEDY and
>MACKENZIE sip on them while they
>dance.)

MACKENZIE
This is so much fun. Can we invite him now?

KENNEDY
(Slurs)
He texted me. He said he was tired.

MACKENZIE

Boo. More drinks?

KENNEDY

I gotta pee. Get more when I come back.

>*(MACKENZIE smiles widely and*
>*continues dancing. She pulls out her*
>*phone and sends a message. Theo's*
>*phone buzzes. He responds quickly.*
>*KENNEDY trails to the bathroom.*
>*She struggles going into the stall, but*
>*emerges soon after. She washes her*
>*hands and pulls out her lipstick out*
>*of her clutch. She reapplies it. She*
>*notices a message on her phone.)*

KENNEDY
(To self)

Stop texting me.

>*(She sets the phone down on the side*
>*of the sink.)*

He has some nerve. "I'm sorry." Haha.

>*(She picks up her phone and begins*
>*typing a text)*

You are a meanie. You broke me. Broke. I'm moving. Out.
Asshole. Seeeend.

>*(She laughs, setting her phone down.*
>*She points at the mirror.)*

You are strong. You can do this. Haha. You looooove him.

>*(She starts sobbing)*

He doesn't love you though. Nope. Look at you. How
could he? Your eyes are not right. Too dead. That lipstick
too much.

(She takes the lipstick out of her clutch again and starts drawing on her face in the mirror.)

He'd like you better like this. Haha wouldn't he? Haha. More drinks.

(KENNEDY exits the bathroom. She bumps into MACKENZIE and they both go to the bar.)

MACKENZIE

What took you so long silly?

KENNEDY

Line.

MACKENZIE

He's coming!

KENNEDY

No. No he isn't. You're drunk.

MACKENZIE

I'm just tipsy. *I can handle my liquor.*

(THEO enters. He scans the crowd.)

KENNEDY

I gotta pee again.

MACKENZIE

You broke the seal! Go. I see him.

(MACKENZIE and THEO are chatting at the bar. KENNEDY goes outside rather than the bathroom.

Everything ensues behind her, but in silence.)

KENNEDY

I hate myself.

KENNEDY
(V.O.)

This piece is from my lowest times. This piece was one of the biggest contributors to the theme of my recent works. Demeaning. In this piece, I was taking away meaning. In the next piece you will see how I explored being degraded, or how I took away meaning from someone else. The next artist will be Jackson Pollock. Continue to his piece *Convergence*. Press 1-0-6 to hear more.

ALMA

Something is off. You barely put any heart into that voice over.

ACT I
SCENE VI

ALMA

I'm starting to think that there is no relation between you and these other artists. You know, I spent 20 dollars to see this exhibit and I'm following your story. I could have taken this time to look at the cool graffiti artist they are featuring in this gallery. But this is the last one. I'm still here. Alright. 2-0-5.

> *(MARIE is smoking a cigarette. She is not as put together as in past scenes. Years have past and it shows in her worn clothes and graying hair. MARIE sits on the edge of the bed as PEYTON plays his/her video game. KENNEDY knocks on the door of the hotel room.)*

KENNEDY

Mom! Mom, open the damn door!

MARIE

God damn girl! Chill. What do you want?

KENNEDY

You're going to be late for your interview.

MARIE

I'm not going. I have to clean these hotel rooms.

KENNEDY

You need a job that pays you.

MARIE

This is just fine.

KENNEDY

Get up. Help mom do the rooms.

PEYTON

Why?

KENNEDY

She has a job interview.

PEYTON

So?

KENNEDY

Did you apply to school yet? We started the application.
Come on!

PEYTON

It's too expensive.

KENNEDY

That's what financial aid is for.

MARIE

I've been riding Peyton's ass to finish.

KENNEDY

Mom, just get ready for the interview. We will finish the
rooms.

MARIE

If your father paid the child support, we wouldn't have to
work so fucking hard.

KENNEDY

Come on mom. You know it's not like that.

MARIE

Whatever. Where is this damn interview?

KENNEDY
(V.O.)

My mom was stubborn, but she knew. You can see the different scenes of her struggle in this piece. (*Tiredly*) Please continue on to the next and final piece of the exhibit. Press 2-0-6.

ACT I
SCENE VII

ALMA

So this is the last painting, huh? Humiliating? Why don't
you tell me about it then? 2-0-6.

*(THEO and KENNEDY enter their
apartment.)*

THEO

That space was awesome. Do you think you'll ask the
owner to buy it?

KENNEDY

I don't know. The other hostel has been doing great. I'm
just not sure I can manage another one.

THEO

You can always hire someone to manage and oversee the
renovations at that property.

KENNEDY

True.

THEO

That space just had it all and if you could get the other level
of that warehouse. You could double your clients!

KENNEDY

Calm down. Go work on those manuscripts.

*(THEO goes to another part of the
stage. He picks up a box and eyes it.
It's clear it's a box with a wedding
ring. He sets it back down as he*

reads over the manuscripts. He gets up unable to focus and goes back to the kitchen where KENNEDY is sitting.)

THEO

Hey?

KENNEDY

Don't even bring it up again. You know I can't afford it on my own.

THEO

It's not about the hostel.

KENNEDY

You should be working. Those manuscripts are due soon.

THEO

I love you, you know.

KENNEDY

Of course, I know.

THEO

Are you ever going to change your mind?

KENNEDY

About loving you?

THEO

No. About…

KENNEDY

Marriage? You know how I feel about that.

THEO

We've been together for a while now.

KENNEDY

A while?

THEO

Babe.

KENNEDY

Don't say that. We're not in college anymore.

THEO

Are you sure everything is alright?

KENNEDY

I'm just stressed.

KENNEDY
(V.O.)

And this is the last piece in this exhibition. I am glad you could take the time to enjoy my work as well as the work of many other local artists and famous artists. For more on the collections, please visit the gift shop at the end of the exhibit.

> *(KENNEDY gets out plates and starts cooking. She puts a pot of boiling water on the stove. She sets the table and then adds the pasta to the pot. KENNEDY opens a cabinet and pulls out a postcard. She starts writing.)*

ALMA

You didn't explain anything!

(ALMA takes off the headphones
and finally picks up a brochure. She
turns it in her hands, reading. She
looks over the last painting one more
time. She looks at her watch
panicked.)

He is going to kill me! I'm going to be late!

(ALMA runs out of the gallery.)

(Black out)

ACT I
SCENE VIII

(Curtains closed. THEO paces the stage. We hear the sound of a train station announcement. THEO dodges people as they come past him. He is waiting for someone.)

ALMA

THEO!

THEO

Alma! Long time no see.

>   *(They hug and THEO takes Alma's bags.)*

ALMA

How is my favorite cousin?

THEO

Great. Can't believe it's been four years!

ALMA

Well, I've gotten a lot smarter since my high school graduation.

THEO

Oh Miss I've got a B.A. now!

ALMA

Actually a M.A.

THEO

No way!

ALMA

If somebody was on Facebook, he would know.

THEO

Well, you'll have plenty of time to tell me.

ALMA

Are you sure your girlfriend is alright with me crashing for a month?

THEO

Ex-girlfriend. We have a spare room. It will help with rent.

ALMA

Ex-girlfriend? Dude, I thought you were going to be engaged by the time I got here! I was ready to celebrate.

THEO

Well she said no. Like hell no.

ALMA

So she still lives there?

THEO

It's complicated. Tell me about your trip here! Come on I want to hear about this cross country train ride.

ALMA

Fine.

ACT I
SCENE IV

(KENNEDY is working at the table while dinner cooks. THEO and ALMA enter goofing off.)

ALMA

See you should have visited me in California!

THEO

You know I was busy.

ALMA

Busy kissing ass to people who still are not promoting you?

KENNEDY

Sounds about right.

ALMA

You must be Kennedy! I've heard a lot about you.

(Goes in for a hug, but Kennedy steps away.)

KENNEDY

Alma? Theo's younger cousin?

ALMA

C'est moi.

THEO

Still as spunky and annoying as when we were kids.

KENNEDY

I see that. Dinner is almost ready.

THEO

What are you making?

KENNEDY

Just spaghetti and meatballs.

THEO

A classic from the red elephant.

ALMA

Red elephant?

KENNEDY

It's a nickname from when I was a kid.

ALMA

That's weird. That rings a bell.

KENNEDY

I was a bit over imaginative as a kid.

THEO

Now all she does is work, work, work.

KENNDY

Seriously?

THEO

It's so she can buy her own hostel.

ALMA

That's neat.

KENNEDY

Come on. Let's all sit for dinner.

(KENNEDY plates the food and they all sit down. ALMA digs for a bottle of wine.)

ALMA

We picked this up on the way in. I would have brought some from California, but it broke somewhere between here and there on the train.

THEO

So you're both klutzes?

ALMA

You know you are an asshole?

KENNEDY

See your cousin agrees.

THEO

Well, dinner smells amazing. Thanks for cooking…

ALMA

Still rough around the edges (ALMA punches THEO) Aren't you like 30 now? Shouldn't you know better?

THEO

29.

ALMA

Still an old man in my book.

KENNEDY

You guys must have been close.

ALMA

His mom babysat me all the time. We were like siblings.

THEO

Celebrated everything together. Christmas. Thanksgiving.
Birthdays.

ALMA

All that nonsense.

KENNDY

Nice. So your room is almost ready. I just have to move
one more box.

ALMA

It's no rush. Theo said it was a spare room.

KENNEDY

It's actually my old room. I'm hoping to find a place in the
next two weeks. I'm busy at the hostel anyways working.
I'll stay there and on the couch.

ALMA

Seriously?

KENNEDY

Yeah.

THEO

We should eat. Why don't you tell us about your way in?

ALMA

Well, I just came from Philly.

THEO

That's where Kennedy's mom lives.

KENNEDY

What did you do there? I miss it back home sometimes. Not as crazy as New York.

ALMA

I went to the Philly Museum. Wanted to run the Rocky steps. See the exhibits. Almost missed my train. (ALMA digs in her bag and pulls out the brochure and throws it at Theo. He scans it over and hands in to Kennedy)

THEO

Hannah Shay? That's funny. Your middle name is Hannah. And your last name is Shay.

KENNEDY

What a coincidence. Strange.

ALMA

Oh shit. You're the artist in the exhibit. Red elephant in the room.

KENNEDY

I don't know what you are talking about.

THEO

Kennedy has never been on exhibit. Right? I thought you gave up on that.

ALMA

I didn't get a Masters in journalism for nothing. It makes so much sense. Didn't you tell me that Kennedy lived and grew up in Philly?

THEO

Yeah.

KENNEDY

Can I see that?

THEO

Sure.

KENNEDY

This isn't me.

ALMA

It is. Look you're sweating. You're nervous.

KENNEDY

Shut up! (The plate falls on to her lap)

THEO

See? Red elephant.

ALMA

I suppose it's a good thing you and my cousin didn't get engaged.

KENNEDY

You told her I said no?

THEO

She asked.

KENNEDY

It was a year ago.

ALMA

This is a bit awkward. I thought you said you still had the ring you dimwit!

KENNEDY

I'm going to go change.

THEO

Kennedy. Wait. Why didn't you tell me? This is great. We always use to dream about making it big and look (grabbing brochure, rambling)

KENNEDY

You don't know anything about me.

(KENNEDY exits. Upset.)

THEO

Kennedy.

ALMA

I wouldn't follow her.

THEO

Things are complicated, Alma.

ALMA

Apparently.

THEO

This isn't the time to be a smart ass.

ALMA

So you wanna go to Philly this weekend?

(THEO eyerolls and follows
KENNEDY off stage. ALMA shrugs
and sits back at the table to eat her
spaghetti.)
(BLACK OUT)

ACT I
SCENE X
(KENNEDY is alone in the gallery looking at the
artwork on the walls. The set should be high contrast
between bright white and dark. There should be a blank
canvas or sheet in the center.On the wall should be
Cezzane's The Bathers, Van Gogh's Starry Night,
Picasso's Girl Before a Mirror, Kahlo's Two Fridays,
Pollock's Convergence.)

*(THE ARTISTS enter each with a sheet One by one as they
enter they cover their own paintings with a painted sheet.
These should be representative of the scenes previously
viewed by Alma.They can be abstract or literal.)*

*(MARIE, JOSEPH, PEYTON, and MACKENZIE walk in
either covered in paint or in tight costumes that have a lot
of texture and color similar to a painting.)*

*(THEO walks in in all white carrying paint and a
paintbrush. Pauses with it between him and Kennedy. He
hesitantly hands her the paint brush and stands by the
blank canvas. ALMA enters from the audience. Kennedy
has now moved to center stage. Alma walks behind her and
pulls a cloth of a photography portrait of Kennedy. The
photography post gradually drips to look like paint as the
ensemble slowly moves off stage leaving Kennedy alone to
look at the portrait of herself.)*

(Blackout.)

ACT II
SCENE I

(THEO exits the Philadelphia Museum Exhibition flipping the brochure for Kennedy's exhibit in his hands. ALMA exits soon after. Note that the stage should be set similar to the beginning of Act 1, though the transition will not be into a frame, but will transition into a blank white wall.)

THEO
Do you think people know that was me?

ALMA
No. It's not like she painted a picture perfect portrait of you.

THEO
Why wouldn't she tell me about this?

ALMA
I don't know. Her life in New York is so different than her life here.

THEO
I called her mom. Apparently Kennedy has a studio in the garage of her mom's house.

ALMA
I thought her mom was living in a hotel.

THEO
Alma, that's just one memory. It's complicated. You wouldn't understand.

ALMA

I just saw her pour her heart out across canvases. I think I get her a little bit.

THEO

It's just art.

ALMA

And this is why she probably didn't tell you.

THEO

What do you mean? I know Kennedy like the back of my hand. We dated for five years! I've seen her art before!

ALMA

You're blind. I can't believe you two have been living together for a year since she said no.
> *(ALMA snatches the brochure from him. She finds the piece of work she is looking for.)*

Look. See this spill right here. It's not just a spill.

THEO

Rent is expensive in New York! It is just a spill (*Theo looks at the brochure again*) She even said that in the audio guide. Were you even listening?

ALMA

God. It didn't just spill. She threw it at the painting. She was angry. You can tell by the way it splattered. If it would have just spilled, it'd be cleaner around the edges. Like a puddle. But look, splatters everywhere.

THEO

You have a good point. But it's just a painting. Maybe she was just mad because she couldn't capture something

ALMA

You are a writer. Right?

THEO

Editor.

ALMA

Whatever. I know you write. You used to tell me all those stories when we were kids! Don't you ever just write a shitty chapter? Something melodramatic? Something to just get your emotions out?

THEO

Of course.

ALMA

It's the same thing for Kennedy.

THEO

How can you say that? You don't even know her?

ALMA

I don't have to know her to know that. It's all in the paint. Just like it's all in the words of a book. You are a good listener but a terrible observer. Now, let's get food. I'm starving. You're paying.

THEO

But...

ALMA

Come on! We don't have all day.

THEO

Let me just call Kennedy quick.

ALMA

Fine. But I'm going outside.

(ALMA exits)

(THEO dials Kennedy's number and paces the stage.)

(A spotlight shines on KENNEDY. A light projects a video on the walls, indicating she is in an airport. She pulls out her phone and looks at the screen.)

KENNEDY

Hey Theo. You went, didn't you?

THEO

Of course.

KENNEDY

I thought so.

THEO

I wanted to see the exhibit.

KENNEDY

I know.

THEO

Where are you anyways?

KENNEDY

Where do you think I am? I'm at the hostel. It's just busy around here today. It started raining so people didn't want to go out into the city.

THEO

Didn't think it was supposed to rain today?

KENNEDY

It's just pouring out there.

THEO

I swear I heard an announcement for a plane. Are you at JFK?

KENNEDY

Why would I be at JFK, Theo? You know how busy the hostel is this weekend.

THEO

Yeah. That's crazy. I wanted to tell you I thought the exhibit was great. I loved all of your stories. Your technique was great.

KENNEDY

My technique?

THEO

Yeah. It was very…well formed.

KENNEDY

It's not writing.

THEO

Kennedy. I'm…

KENNEDY

I don't expect you to understand.

THEO

I want to though.

KENNEDY
Theo, I have to go soon.

THEO
Your works. They made me think a lot. A lot about us.

KENNEDY
Don't worry about it. You don't have to get all sentimental about our past right now.

THEO
Yeah. I guess so. I just wanted to tell you…I wanted to congratulate you on this exhibit. I'm proud of you.

KENNEDY
I have to go. There is…there is a predicament at the hostel.

THEO
I'll see you tonight.

KENNEDY
See you…tonight.

(KENNEDY hangs up the phone. MACKENZIE rushes up to her waving her passport.)

MACKENZIE
Ready?

KENNEDY
Ready.

(THEO holds the phone in his hand, pacing. He pauses then exits. The

stage darkens. A sound of train station announcements particular to Philadelphia and New York Penn Station are heard as well as sounds from an airline. Announcements to fasten seat belts are heard in English and Spanish.)

(The stage lights up when THEO opens the door. A small light is focused on a note on the table. The apartment is quiet. Theo sets his bag down, turning on a few more lights.)

THEO

Kennedy? Kennedy, do you just want to order out?

ALMA

Theo.

(Holding up the note. THEO grabs it from her.)

THEO

What does this mean?

ALMA

I don't know. I didn't read it.

THEO

Dear Theo, Don't worry. I'm with Mackenzie. When I come back, I will be moving out. Adios, Kennedy.

ALMA

With Mackenzie? That's her traveling friend right?

THEO

She is moving out.

ALMA

That's what you are worried about.

THEO

I guess I thought I had more time. It's not like things really changed.

ALMA

You are literally not a couple? Living in two different rooms…

THEO

Well. Kind of.

ALMA

This is why I don't date. Why don't you just call Mackenzie?

THEO

Mackenzie doesn't have a permanent phone anymore. She only writes letters when she is traveling. You never know where she is until she sends you a postcard and by then she has moved on.

ALMA

I'm sure Kennedy will be back.

THEO

You don't know her.

ALMA

Let's find her.

THEO

Find her?

ALMA

Why not? I'm sure Mr. Big Shot Editor can get some time off.

THEO

That's beside the point.

ALMA

We will follow the paintings.

THEO

She didn't leave clues in the paintings.

ALMA

So?

THEO

So?

ALMA

Don't you want to see the things she talked about? The places she grew up? Talk to her dad. Talk to her mom.

THEO

I've met her mom.

ALMA

Come on. Don't you have any adventure in your blood! I could write a piece about this. I could practice my photography.

THEO

I have to work! And don't you have to find a job.

ALMA

Blah blah blah. Just think! You can learn more about the love of your life. I can take some photos. I can write my next big article. And you can write all about it too! From your perspective. Whatever that is.

THEO

Love of my life?

ALMA

Don't scoff at me. Maybe I do root for romance. Plus, you have that lost puppy look.

THEO

I don't have a look.

ALMA

Yeah. Whatever. So first place first…
(Alma pulls out a book of the exhibition)

THEO

What makes you think an adventure will inspire me?

ALMA

You are so dense. Spontaneity…is inspiring! Now…first place…Clarion County.

THEO

How do you suppose we get there? I'm a New Yorker. I don't have a car.

ALMA

That's true. Well maybe we can just call her dad and ask him some questions. I'm sure he knows how to FaceTime.

THEO

I don't know his phone number.

ALMA

Well we can "pack" things up for Kennedy and find it there.

THEO

I don't think going through her stuff is the answer. Why are you so driven to do this anyways?

ALMA

Maybe I want to help my favorite cousin fix his love life. Maybe I need something to write about. AND maybe I'm hella curious. You have a problem with that?

THEO

Yes. Lots of problems with that.

ALMA

You know I always win.

THEO

I know. That's why I am going to look for the stupid phone number.

ALMA

You're the best, Theo!

> *(THEO huffs defeated. ALMA takes a slip of paper out of her bag and starts paging through the exhibition book. Writing things down.)*

ACT II
SCENE II

(ALMA is sprawled out on the floor. Theo is pacing. Alma gets up and sits at the table. Finally THEO sits down.)

THEO
Alright. Here's the number.

ALMA
Alright. Are you nervous?

THEO
Nervous?

ALMA
You never met her dad. Do you think she has told him about you?

THEO
I don't know.

ALMA
I'm nervous.

THEO
Ms. Sassypants is nervous!

ALMA
Shut up. What if he won't talk to us?

THEO
All we can do is try and dial. Did you leave a voicemail last night like you said?

ALMA

Yea.

THEO

Alright. Here. It's 814-226-8721.

ALMA

Slower!

THEO

8-1-4-2-2-6-8-7-2-1.

ALMA

Okay okay it's ringing.

THEO

Put it on speaker.

(Beat between phone rings)

Kennedy told me about her house once. She said that she always hated how the white paint peeled off her house. She didn't talk about what it was like.

JOSEPH

Hello?

ALMA

Shhh! It's him. Say something.

JOSEPH

Hello? Is this Theo?

THEO

Uh. Yes. Sir it's me. And my cousin, Alma.

JOSEPH

Theo? That name sounds familiar.

ALMA

I'm Alma. Theo is your daughter's roommate/lover/ex-fiance.

THEO

Alma!

ALMA

Well it's the truth.

JOSEPH

Okay. Okay. So why are you calling? Are you calling to ask permission to marry her? I'm confused. I thought you two were done? I couldn't quite understand the voicemail if I'm being honest.

THEO

It's complicated.

ALMA

We are calling because we are trying to find Kennedy.

JOSEPH

Find Kennedy? What do you mean?

THEO

She isn't missing. She is with Mackenzie. God Alma, don't scare the man.

JOSEPH

I see. It's so hard to contact Mackenzie.

ALMA
(*Fastly*)
Well, she had this amazing exhibit in the Philadelphia
Museum of Art. But she kept it a secret in New York from
my cousin. So we are trying to figure out why? I'm a
budding journalist.

JOSEPH
You have to slow down.

ALMA
I'm just looking for answers.

JOSEPH
And Theo, why are you going along with this? The way
Kennedy described you, you weren't the one for all this. I
wish we could meet in person sometime. I've heard so
much about you.

THEO
Well, I highly doubt that will happen. Kennedy is moving
out or not coming back.

JOSEPH
Moving out? I don't think that is right. I just spoke with
her. We were actually planning a time where I could take a
train to Philly to see the exhibit.

ALMA
Joseph or can I call you Joe, Joe...can we FaceTime? I
think that is the best we can do for meeting face to face at
this time. I'd really like to see that painting Kennedy did
for you. She talked about it in her exhibit and I wanted to
see it.

JOSEPH

Uhm. I suppose so. I really am no good at technology, but Kennedy did show me once. Hold on.

(There is a moment of silence as JOSEPH figures out how to turn on video call.)

ALMA

This is amazing.

THEO

Can't believe we are bothering Kennedy's dad.

ALMA

You ruin all the fun. Lighten up.

JOSEPH

I got it. Wow! Look at you two! You guys look like brother and sister. It's nice to finally actually see you, Theo. I've heard a lot about you.

ALMA
(mutters)

Probably a lot of bitching.

JOSEPH

Oh no. She always talked highly of Theo. She loves you. Though I suppose like you said it's complicated. Love always is.

ALMA

I have a lot of questions.

JOESPH

I suppose I should have known that by now.

THEO

I'm sorry if we are a bother.

JOESPH

It's not a problem. I've quite the soft spot for you. I'm sorry Kennedy didn't accept your proposal.

THEO

Well, I shouldn't have pushed it.

ALMA

This isn't a therapy session. So Joe can you just tell us a little about Clarion. The house. Oh and can you show me the painting?

JOESPH

It's over here. Let me show you.
(beat)
When I met her mother... We were so young then. We loved that little diner. It was the only exciting place in Clarion. She was a waitress and she would be the only one roller-skating. (*Laughs*) One night, I waited for her shift to be over and I drove her home. One thing led to another. Kennedy was born nine months after. Marie really admired Jackie O's style, but we wanted something a bit different. So we went with Kennedy. A year later, we got married. We learned to love each other I guess. But, it was rocky. But we tried to make it work. I loved her. We had Peyton three years later. It helped. We did more family things. Visited our parents. Even went to Disney. The kids loved it. But she started sleeping with our mechanic regularly. She was getting drunk a lot. She wasn't happy here. I was trying to save to move, but I couldn't get the money with the way all the businesses were closing. There's the old home improvement store. I drive a bit now to work. It keeps me stable and happy.

ALMA

Are you dating anyone new?

JOSEPH

Haha. No. I'm happier alone. I'm a proud dad. I can't
blame Marie for what happened. We didn't love each other.
It wasn't going to work and it was better for us to go
separate ways. I send whatever I can to the family. I'm
happy here though.

ALMA

Did you know about Kennedy's exhibit?

JOSEPH

Of course. I tried to get her to tell Theo. She didn't want to.

ALMA

Why not?

JOSEPH

She told me he wouldn't understand. She is a driven girl. I
let her decide her path.

THEO

Do you think she is really embarrassed of her past?

JOSEPH

No. She just takes a bit of work.

THEO

Why do you think she hid the exhibit from me?

JOSEPH

I don't know.
(beat)
It's getting pretty late for this old guy.

ALMA

Thank you for your time, Joseph.

JOSEPH

You tell my daughter to write to me as soon as she is back from her shenanigans with Mackenzie.

ALMA

I sure will!

JOSEPH

Don't worry Theo. She runs from what she loves.

THEO

Yeah. It was nice talking with you. Maybe we will get to meet sometime.

JOSEPH

Better invite me to that wedding when it happens.

THEO

I don't think Kennedy is one for weddings. Or marriage.

JOSEPH

True. You'll have to visit when you want some time away from the city. I want you two here for dinner once. Or well three. You are welcome to join Alma, if you are around.

THEO

Will do. Good night, Joseph.

ALMA

Good night!
                    (Hangs up phone call.)
Now. Write something. I'm going out on the town. I feel so liberated.

THEO

What?

ALMA

Humor me. Write something. I still have too many
questions. And I'm too young to go to bed right now. Look
at you, you're yawning.

THEO

Alright. Alright. I'll write. Enjoy your night on the town.

ACT II
SCENE III

(ALMA and THEO are on a train toward Philly. Both working on respective work.)

ALMA

Read what you have.

THEO

It's not right yet. Plus we are almost to Philly.

ALMA

What if Kennedy is in Philly?

THEO

She isn't.

ALMA

How do you know?

THEO

I know her.

ALMA

Are you worried?

THEO

Yeah...

ALMA

Why did you guys break up anyways?

THEO

I don't know. We both had a bad day. Tension was high already because one of my exes was in town and...I was

stupid and got drinks with her. Nothing happened. Kennedy
was stressed because the hostel was falling apart. She just
started managing it then. We started fighting over dinner.
She blamed me for going out because she said no to my
proposal.

ALMA

You broke up over one fight?

THEO

I suppose so. We had fought before. It wasn't out of the
ordinary.

ALMA

So why did you end it?

THEO

Just because some audio guide Kennedy told you I ended it
doesn't mean I did.

ALMA

So she ended it?

THEO

Yeah. She handed me back the engagement ring one day
over breakfast. Said we should see other people.

ALMA

Why didn't she move out?

THEO

You sure ask a lot of questions. Come on. It's time to get
off the train.

ALMA

Just answer the question.

THEO

(*Laughs*)

She asked me if she could stay. Rent was figured out, groceries, the works. Ya know?

ALMA

Did you end up seeing other people?

THEO

Only two dates. A month later. I mean…they weren't her though.

ALMA

Look who's a bit sappy.

THEO

Not fair. The uber is over there. I texted her mom that we will be there shortly.

ALMA

What's she really like?

THEO

Kennedy?

ALMA

Yeah.

THEO

She is a bit goofy. Smart. She is always looking out for everyone else, but never herself. She's that girl poets write about. Mysterious, but…she's a hard girl to put into words.

ALMA

You should write it down. Or at least…try to capture her.

THEO

I've tried. Getting her right on paper…just never can quite capture her.

ALMA

That's why you have writer's block.

THEO

Whatever. Now…before we go in. Are you going to tell me what's going on?

ALMA

That's not important.

THEO

Come on. You know I can tell there is something off.

ALMA

I don't know.

THEO

You thought you'd have a job by now didn't you?

ALMA

I suppose. Sometimes I wonder if I chose the right path.

THEO

You know I know journalists.

ALMA

I couldn't ask you for a job. I want to earn it.

THEO

There's nothing wrong with getting a little help.

ALMA

You did it on your own.

THEO

I went to school in New York. I worked long hours. I met people. It wasn't just luck.

ALMA

So you are telling me you didn't just magically get hired at a big editing firm?

THEO

Not at all. Actually it was someone Kennedy met. She told them about me and she gave them some of my work in the NYU paper.

ALMA

Really?

THEO

When I had to work an unpaid internship, it was Kennedy's couch I stayed on. It was four of us. Mackenzie slept on an air mattress. Kennedy had a boyfriend then. I slept on the couch.

ALMA

Wait. What?

THEO

Yeah. I worked at a coffee shop right by the apartment.

ALMA

No. Kennedy had a boyfriend and you were sleeping on her couch.

THEO
There was a lot I didn't tell my mom and your mom when I came home for breaks. We were all young college kids just trying to live out our dreams in New York. It was what you did. Come on let's go in. I can smell dinner.

ALMA
Surprised you actually sounded like you had fun once in your life.

(THEO knocks on the door. MARIE greets him with a huge hug)

MARIE
Theo! You made it. Is this that crazy cousin you said was coming with you?

ALMA
You told her I was crazy?

THEO
Yes. Yes. I did.

MARIE
It's okay. We are all a bit crazy. I mean…look at this one over here. (*nudges Theo*)

THEO
Hey! Not fair!

MARIE
Still my favorite ex-son-in-law.

THEO
I never made it to son-in-law (*laughs but Marie nudges him*) How's Peyton doing?

MARIE

Good. Good. Ya know they promoted her down at the grocery store? My little kid is an assistant manager now!

THEO

That's great.

MARIE

Honey, so ya know college isn't for everyone. Peyton is making good money and she doesn't have a college degree. It took her some time...well too damn long actually...to figure it out. But she did. She figured it out.

THEO

Now to get them their own place.

MARIE

Right? This girl has to get her party on.

ALMA

I bet you throw the craziest parties on the block.

MARIE

You know it. I'm the craziest bitch on this block and damn well proud of it.

ALMA

You are not all what I expected.

MARIE

It's because you saw that exhibit. Kennedy warned me. But they didn't include all her work and all her audio.

THEO

I told you, you didn't know what you think you know.

MARIE

You'd think this one is your older brother with the way he
teases ya.

ALMA

I'm secretly his favorite cousin. But he has problems
admitting things.

MARIE

Tell me about it! You know how long it took him to finally
ask my daughter out on a real date. Come on inside. Let me
introduce you to Peyton.

ALMA

So how long did it take you to ask her out?

THEO

I don't understand why you are so preoccupied with my
relationship with her.

MARIE

She is a fucking young girl. Some of us girls still believe in
all that cheesy love stuff ya know.

THEO
(*sighs*)
It took me about a year. But to my defense, we were friends
and as I said she just got out of a relationship. It was a big
risk.

MARIE

You know she is gonna ask how you two met. So you
might as well tell her.

(PEYTON enters.)

PEYTON

Theo! How are you man?

THEO

Good. Congrats on the job!

PEYTON

Yeah it's a pretty sweet jig. Where's Kennedy? Is this your new girlfriend?

THEO and ALMA

Ew.

ALMA

No. I'm Alma. Theo's cousin.

> *(PEYTON and ALMA shake hands.)*

PEYTON

Alma. Nice. My girlfriend is Spanish and she always says: *tienes una alma buena*. No wonder why you are so spunky! Your name translates to soul.

ALMA

Yup. My parents had a thing for powerful names. I got a sister named Destiny. Now that's a name with shoes to fill.

PEYTON

Makes me glad my name is just Peyton. So what's the reason for the trip Theo?

THEO

Well, Kennedy left me a note saying she was with Mackenzie and she was moving out. I was a bit worried.

PEYTON

Worried enough to travel here? I know you are like family
here, but you have a busy work schedule. So Kennedy
always said when you couldn't come.

MARIE

Kennedy isn't missing though. She is just traveling with
Mackenzie.

PEYTON

They were only going to like…

MARIE
(*interrupts*)
Who cares where they are traveling? Kennedy just needs a
break from things.

THEO

Do you know where they are?

MARIE

Not going to lie to you. I do. But I promised her I wouldn't
give in to your handsome face. But I do have some things
to show you.

ALMA

Really?

MARIE

Yeah. You'll like this. Let's go back to her studio. She
figured with this one's spirit, you'd end up here at some
point.

THEO

I think I might try to give her a call.

ALMA

Come on. You can try again later. You want to understand her art, right?

> *(THEO shakes his head, but follows. The cast stands upstage as Marie chats and points. Theo attempting to paint a portrait. The scene fades. Beat. Fades back to day to show passing of time.)*

Thanks so much Marie! And thanks for showing me this side of Philly!

MARIE

It's no problem.

ALMA

We will see you again hopefully.

ACT II
SCENE IV

(THEO and ALMA enter. Yawning.)

THEO

Home sweet home.

ALMA

I suppose.

THEO

Come on. Let's go get some coffee in the city. There are still some things you have to see.

ALMA

Did my adventurous spirit finally rub off on you?

THEO
(*Teasingly*)

Oh no way.

ALMA

Why are you smiling like that?

THEO

Because I have an idea.

ALMA

I've created a monster.

(*ALMA and THEO go off stage briefly and return with Starbucks*)

THEO

Best coffee in all of New York!

ALMA

But this is Starbucks…

THEO

But this Starbucks! Best one. Hands down.

ALMA

I'm guessing your "struggling writer" syndrome gives you
the right to make that claim?

THEO

Hell yes!

ALMA

So what's your big idea? I'm on a deadline so you know.

THEO

Adventures have no deadline.

ALMA

Touché.

THEO

I wanted to show you the places in New York that are
important from the exhibit.

ALMA

Okay?

THEO

That's not all.

ALMA

Well don't keep me hanging!

THEO

You don't know everything yet.

ALMA

What do you mean? We just met her family!

THEO

Yeah, but if you knew Kennedy you'd know that family isn't just her blood relations.

ALMA

So what am I missing?

THEO

Me and Mackenzie. And more stories about Kennedy.

ALMA

Well I know you.

THEO

Yeah. When we were kids. We haven't seen each other in four years.

ALMA

Fine. You're right. But how will this help us find Kennedy?

THEO

I know where she is.

ALMA

No you don't.

THEO
(*pulls out the note*)
Adios. She is in Spain.

ALMA

You know there is more than one country that speaks Spanish?

THEO

I know. But check this out...

(THEO pulls out last month's Conde Nast Traveller and flips to a page)

ALMA

"Cities You Might Have Missed: Some of our favorite travel writers are bringing you to the cities that inspired them to hit the road and never look back. Next month, our special edition will be cover to cover inspiration."

THEO

Think of the exhibit!

ALMA

Are you telling me that Mackenzie is just as obsessed with Spain as Kennedy?

THEO

It's Mackenzie's favorite place and she wouldn't write an inspired travel piece without her best friend.

ALMA

I can't go to Spain. We don't have time. And I can't afford a last minute ticket!

THEO

Don't freak out. I bought tickets already. We leave tomorrow at 6:00.

ALMA

How?

THEO

Mr. Big Shot Editor has connections…and a boss who
wants to read a manuscript.

ALMA

You've been sharing your writing?

THEO

No. I just sent him a short email with some quips. Telling
him I'd be back in the office soon. He wanted to know
more about this story…so I told him and next thing I knew,
two tickets to Spain were in my email box.

ALMA

So your boss figured out where she was?

THEO

It did help that he knew Mackenzie's itinerary…he knows
the people over at Conde Nast. He sent me the magazine
and it clicked.

ALMA

Look at you.

THEO

Don't hate me, but I did tell him about you. He wants an
article after.

ALMA

How did you manage to convince him of that? You have no
idea if I'm a good journalist or not.

THEO

You left your phone out. Plus, I googled your name and set him stories from when you were out in Cali.

ALMA

That's not funny.

THEO

Well, it could be a job. And I do have a back up plan or a secondary job.

ALMA

God. Alright. Mr. Full of Ideas.

THEO

Kennedy needs some help at the hostel. She is a bit short staffed.

ALMA

You are talking some big game right now. Where are we walking to anyways?

THEO

Here.

ALMA

Why are we at the NYU bookstore?

THEO

This is where I met Kennedy.

ALMA

You did not meet in a bookstore.

THEO

I sure did. We were both buying books for the same class.
A 500-person class on Intro to Creative Writing.

ALMA

So you and Kennedy are like fucking soul mates!

THEO

Maybe. She met Mackenzie in that dorm over there. I lived
in the hall below them. We eventually all came together
and took on the city together.

ALMA

Why didn't you travel with them?

THEO

I was scared. I'm not a risk taker. That year Mackenzie and
Kennedy spent in Spain…it was hard. I was working at the
publishing house. Getting everyone's coffee. Writing late
in any Starbucks I could find. I thought I had this great
piece of work. My old boss just threw it in the trash. Didn't
even flip a page. I stuck to editing after that. I have piles of
drafts. Kennedy always tried to get me to submit the work
to different literary magazines.

ALMA

But you were too worried about making it big?

THEO

Yup. I missed out on a lot of things working my way to the
top.

ALMA

You were in the original plans to go to Spain. Weren't you?

THEO

Sure was. I thought I'd be like Hemingway. Go to Spain and write some great novels. But I had the job. I had a girlfriend who I thought I was going to marry.

ALMA

Then you realized something.

THEO

Sure did. Isn't that cheesy? Someone goes away and you realize…you realize that you've loved them the whole time.

ALMA

It is a bit cheesy. I would have never thought you would have given up on all that when we were growing up. I looked up to you.

THEO

You did?

ALMA

Of course. I wanted to be just like you. Why do you think I even picked up a pen to begin with?

THEO

I guess I didn't realize.

ALMA

What's Mackenzie like?

THEO

Fireball. I swear you could be her younger sister. She asks a lot of questions. Does what she wants. She walks into a room and owns it. She got a full ride to NYU. She was first generation. She knows what makes her happy. I'm sure she will slap me across the face when she sees me.

ALMA

I wish I had those kinds of friends.

THEO

You are telling me you didn't make any friends out in Cali?

ALMA

I guess. I am not much of a West Coast girl. I couldn't get into it.

THEO

Well, you will make tons of cool friends to rock out the rest of your twenties with here in NYC, even if that means you have to crash with me a bit longer than expected.
(*looks at watch*) We better head back. We have a long flight tomorrow.

ACT II
SCENE V

THEO

Alright. This is us.

ALMA

This city is beautiful. Who would have thought I'd actually make it to Europe?

THEO

Valencia. Just how Kennedy described it. Let's go get some frozen yogurt. (*points*) She always said it was the best. And I could use some food to cool me down. It's a lot warmer here than back home.

ALMA

Same. Where do you think we should look for her?

THEO

I have one place. I'm sure she is there.

> (*THEO and ALMA point at the toppings and things they want. They are handed frozen yogurt.*)

ALMA

You sound hesitant.

THEO

I'm nervous. This is crazy.

ALMA

I think we established that a long time ago.

THEO

All this because of some art exhibit.

ALMA

Yup. Now mmm. This is delicious.

> *(ALMA sits down on a bench and digs into her frozen yogurt. THEO sits down next to Alma and pulls out a map.)*

THEO

There is a café near the university. That's the one she and Mackenzie always were at. She said it was near Mestalla.

ALMA

Mestalla?

THEO

It's where the local football team plays. Here are the universities. There is the stadium. Want to walk there? It's a bit of a walk, but if we just cross this bridge here and go up this avenue. We won't get too lost.

ALMA

Alright. Let's go.

THEO

It's that one.

ALMA

We don't have to go right now if you're not ready.

THEO

We came all this way. No better time than ahora.

ALMA

Qué bueno! Picking up on the Spanish lingo.

THEO

Un poquito.

ALMA

Well…even if she isn't there, I could use a café con leche to deal with this jetlag.

>   *(THEO and ALMA sit down*
>   *at a small table and a waiter*
>   *takes their order. There is a*
>   *small pause as both look*
>   *around for Kennedy.)*

THEO

What if she isn't here? What if we got it all wrong?

ALMA

It's only been an hour. She could be anywhere in the city.

THEO

You're right.

ALMA

What are you going to say to her when you see her?

THEO

I don't know.

ALMA

You get her art more don't you?

THEO

Yea. A lot more.

ALMA

Just not art is it?

THEO

No.

ALMA

She loves you, you know.

THEO

I know. You remember that painting her mom showed us?

ALMA

Yeah of course.

THEO

That one. I've seen it before. I didn't realize it. I saw it on her phone screen.

ALMA

And?

THEO

That one was…that painting was representative of me and her relationship. I could see all the details. I didn't need to hear an audio guide about it to know. I didn't think she loved me as much as I loved her. But it's clear…we both are struggling to capture each other.

ALMA

Look who got all profound.

THEO

Yeah yeah. I know.

ALMA

It's going to be fine.

*(MACKENZIE and KENNEDY
enter.)*

MACKENZIE
(Laughs)

Remember that one time? The time you fell face first in the crosswalk trying to avoid those street jugglers?

KENNEDY

Dear god. Don't remind me. I was just trying to get the bus and bam. The bus driver laughed so hard when I got on.

MACKENZIE

Is that Theo?

KENNEDY

What do you mean? Theo would never come to Spain. He is all work and no play.

MACKENZIE

That's Theo. I swear. *(points)*

KENNEDY

That's not him. It can't be.

MACKENZIE

Hola guapo!!!

*(THEO looks up and waves. A grin
spreads across his face. ALMA turns
around.)*

KENNEDY

Oh no. Fuck no. No Mackenzie. I'm not going over there.

MACKENZIE

Theo came all this way. You know what that means right?

*(MACKENZIE takes KENNEDY by
the arm and they walk to Alma and
Theo. They sit down and wave the
waitress to bring out more cafés.)*

KENNEDY

What are you two doing here?

THEO

We kind of on an assignment? Per se?

KENNEDY

What's that supposed to mean? Why are you guys in
Spain? How?

THEO

My boss. I sent him some blurb and he wanted me to come.
With his help and some other things, we figured out you
were here.

KENNEDY

You sent writing to your boss?

THEO

Finally found the right topic.

ALMA

He needed a little inspiration. And some yelling at.

THEO

She's a bully. Don't let her charm you.

MACKENZIE

Remind me of myself. What's your name again?

ALMA

Alma. You must be Mackenzie.

MACKENZIE

Sure am.

KENNEDY

I just don't understand why you guys came all this way. I
was coming back.

THEO

Part of the adventure was finding you.

KENNEDY

I hope you didn't mean for that to sound as cheesy as it did.

ALMA

He is sappier than he lets on.

THEO

In my defense…

MACKENZIE

Theo, you are incredibly sappy. Don't deny it.

THEO

Fine.

ALMA

So Kennedy…why didn't you finish narrating those last pieces in the exhibit?

KENNEDY

You came all this way and that's your question.

ALMA

I think I know it, but I want your answer.

KENNEDY

The museum didn't have room for the whole story. I did the audio guide for all my pieces, but they picked those ones out. They liked the theme. Humiliation. You think an artist like me would have any say in how they curated my work?

MACKENZIE

They jacked her whole story. It is pretty funny though.

KENNEDY

That's why I didn't want anyone to see it. I told my mom and dad because they were painted in an odd light. No pun intended. I tried to get some more positive pieces in, but they didn't make the cut.

THEO

Was the one in your studio supposed to be there?

KENNEDY

My mom showed you that?

THEO

Yes.

KENNEDY

Yes. That one was supposed to be there too. And the ones at the apartment. I was collecting them in New York. I thought maybe…maybe I could hang them in a private studio somewhere.

ALMA

That'd be fantastic.

KENNEDY

But I want to wait until I have the full story and it sure seems I'd have to add more after this.

THEO

You don't even know.

ALMA

But don't worry! I have ALL the pictures. And I made Theo write it all down.

MACKENZIE

High five girl!

(ALMA and MACKENZIE high five.)

THEO

Want to get a cerveza?

KENNEDY

Sure.

(Alma waves the waitress down excitedly and the waitress brings four beers.)

ALMA
Cheers! Cheers to adventures!

(They all clink glasses, smiling.)

(Blackout.)

ACT II
SCENE VIII

(KENNEDY exits the gallery. She sighs. THEO is waiting at the end. He grabs her hand.)

KENNEDY

Thanks for waiting.

THEO

It's no problem.

KENNEDY

It's weird hearing your own voice talking about your own work.

THEO

I bet.

KENNEDY

It doesn't feel right anymore. People probably think I am someone I am not.

THEO

Well, I know who you are.

KENNEDY

Yeah. How do you think Alma is doing at the hostel?

THEO

According to this text message, I think she is doing just fine.

KENNEDY

She fits in.

THEO

She is something else.

KENNEDY

She is a cool kid.

THEO

Sure is. She told me she is applying to some jobs.

KENNEDY

I guess we aren't getting rid of her anytime soon.

THEO

Mackenzie said she'll mentor her.

KENNEDY

Mackenzie must be thrilled.

THEO

Beyond thrilled.

KENNEDY

I'm sorry.

THEO

For what?

KENNEDY

Breaking us up.

THEO

We are together now.

KENNEDY

I just thought…

THEO

It'd be easier.

KENNEDY

Yeah.

THEO

It's fine. If we didn't, I wouldn't get you like I do now.

KENNEDY

True. Ready to go home?

THEO

Yes. I love you. (*kisses forehead*)

KENNEDY

I love you too.

> *(KENNEDY and THEO exit the gallery.)*

(Blackout.)

ACT II
SCENE IV

(A stage light shines on a bed. THEO gently nudges
KENNEDY awake.)

THEO

You alright babe?

KENNEDY

Yeah. I just had a strange nightmare.

THEO

What about?

KENNEDY

This is going to sound crazy. But all the famous artists in
the exhibit came marching in with the titles of my work on
their canvases. Then all of you guys were like…walking
paintings. You handed me a blank canvas. The portrait then
became a painting.

THEO

That is strange. What do you think it means?

KENNEDY

I don't know.

THEO

Why don't you go back to sleep? It'll be fine. Maybe it's a
sign you should go through with your new exhibit.

KENNEDY

Maybe. I'm going to go get a glass of water. Sleep tight.
(*kisses forehead*)

THEO

Don't stay up too late painting.

KENNEDY

How'd you know?

THEO

You have that look.

KENNEDY

Go to sleep.

(THEO rolls over tiredly as KENNEDY tiptoes to the living room. She props a big canvas up against the wall. It is blank.)

KENNEDY
(V.O.)

Sometimes I hate blank canvases. There is nothing to inspire me. No texture. Nothing that pops out. Other days, I love them. I can come at it in a fresh way. I think how do I show what I'm feeling right now. I feel at peace. Like something is going right. How do I paint that? How do I paint peace when the blank white canvas already says that? Do I make it more chaotic? Will that make my life more chaotic? I don't know. But I pick up the brush anyways. Let the bright red paint drip down. Every story has to start somewhere.

(KENNEDY splashes a big red line of paint across the canvas.)

(End Act II)

End of Play

ACKNOWLEDGEMENTS

Thank you to everyone who has helped me get through this play! Special thanks to those who have continued to encourage me to write and then write some more.

Special thanks to all those who helped with editing this during the Workshop Live event!

Special thanks to my actors who made it through one practice before the COVID-19 pandemic! Fingers crossed we will see this in the future and laugh about it after a successful performance.

Made in the USA
Monee, IL
16 September 2021